ASTERIX AND THE SOOTHSAYER

TEXT BY GOSCINNY

DRAWINGS BY UDERZO

TRANSLATED BY ANTHEA BELL AND DEREK HOCKRIDGE

DARGAUD PUBLISHING INTERNATIONAL, LTD.

ASTERIX THE GAUL	0-917201-50-7
ASTERIX AND THE GOLDEN SICKLE	0-917201-64-7
ASTERIX AND THE GOTHS	0-917201-54-X
ASTERIX THE GLADIATOR	0-917201-55-8
ASTERIX AND THE BANQUET	0-917201-71-X
ASTERIX AND CLEOPATRA	0-917201-75-2
ASTERIX AND THE BIG FIGHT	0-917201-58-2
ASTERIX IN BRITAIN	0-917201-74-4
ASTERIX AND THE NORMANS	0-917201-69-8
ASTERIX THE LEGIONARY	0-917201-56-6
ASTERIX AND THE CHIEFTAIN'S SHIELD	0-917201-67-1
ASTERIX AT THE OLYMPIC GAMES	0-917201-61-2
ASTERIX AND THE CAULDRON	0-917201-66-3
ASTERIX IN SPAIN	0-917201-51-5
ASTERIX AND THE ROMAN AGENT	0-917201-59-0
ASTERIX IN SWITZERLAND	0-917201-57-4
ASTERIX AND THE MANSIONS OF THE GODS	0-917201-60-4
ASTERIX AND THE LAUREL WREATH	0-917201-62-0
ASTERIX AND THE SOOTHSAYER	0-917201-63-9
ASTERIX IN CORSICA	0-917201-72-8
ASTERIX AND CAESAR'S GIFT	0-917201-68-X
ASTERIX AND THE GREAT CROSSING	0-917201-65-5
OBELIX & CO.	0-917201-70-1
ASTERIX IN BELGIUM	0-917201-73-6

ISBN 0-917201-63-9

Exclusive licenced distributor for USA:

Distribooks Inc.
8220 N. Christiana Ave.
Skokie, IL 60076-2911
Tel: (708) 676-1596
Fax: (708) 676-1195
Toll-free fax: 800-433-9229

Imprimé en France-Publiphotoffset 93500 Pantin-en mars 1995

Printed in France

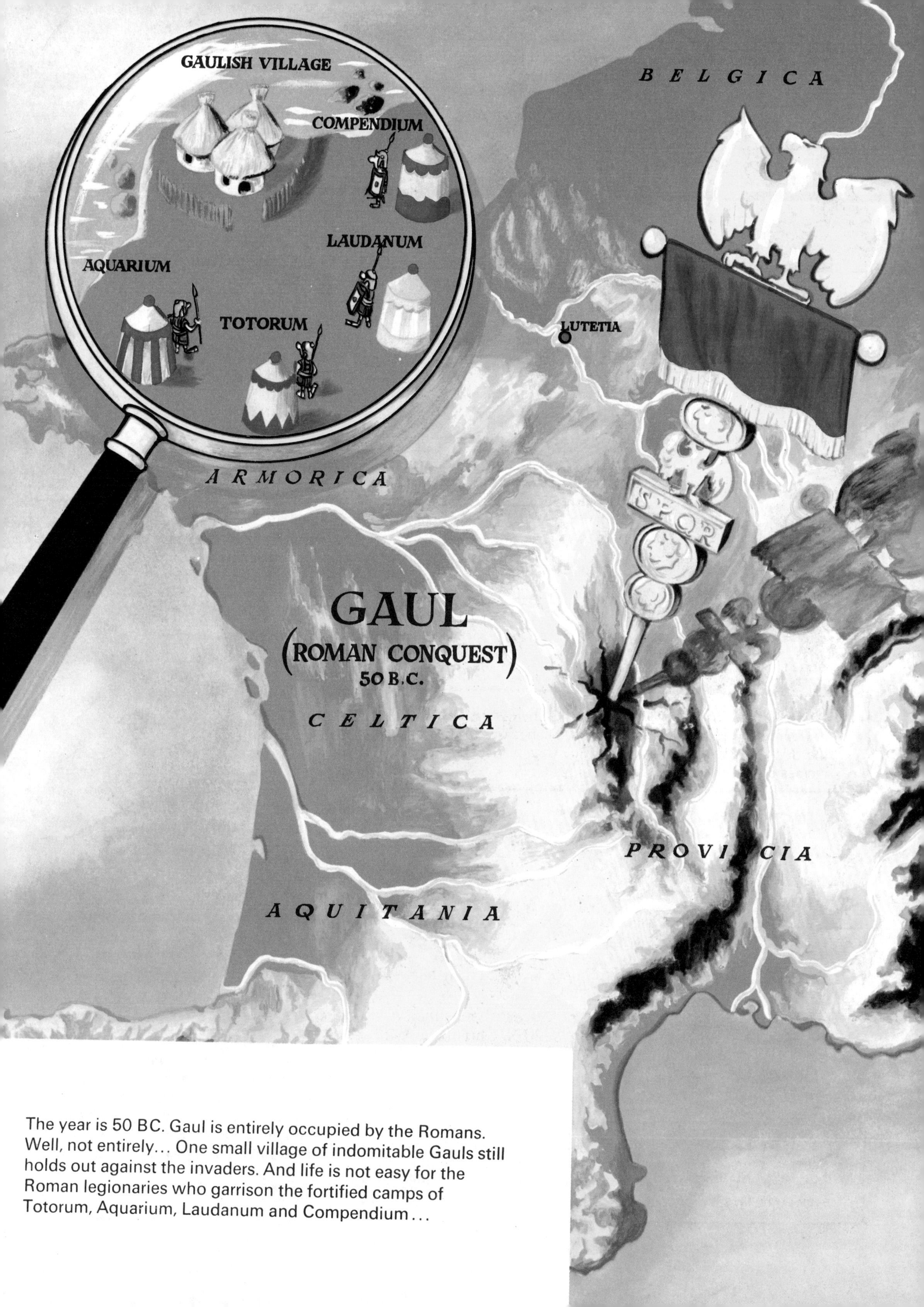

The year is 50 BC. Gaul is entirely occupied by the Romans. Well, not entirely... One small village of indomitable Gauls still holds out against the invaders. And life is not easy for the Roman legionaries who garrison the fortified camps of Totorum, Aquarium, Laudanum and Compendium...

a few of the Gauls

Asterix, the hero of these adventures. A shrewd, cunning little warrior; all perilous missions are immediately entrusted to him. Asterix gets his superhuman strength from the magic potion brewed by the druid Getafix...

Obelix, Asterix's inseparable friend. A menhir delivery-man by trade; addicted to wild boar. Obelix is always ready to drop everything and go off on a new adventure with Asterix – so long as there's wild boar to eat, and plenty of fighting.

Getafix, the venerable village druid. Gathers mistletoe and brews magic potions. His speciality is the potion which gives the drinker superhuman strength. But Getafix also has other recipes up his sleeve...

Cacofonix, the bard. Opinion is divided as to his musical gifts. Cacofonix thinks he's a genius. Everyone else thinks he's unspeakable. But so long as he doesn't speak, let alone sing, everybody likes him...

Finally, Vitalstatistix, the chief of the tribe. Majestic, brave and hot-tempered, the old warrior is respected by his men and feared by his enemies. Vitalstatistix himself has only one fear; he is afraid the sky may fall on his head tomorrow. But as he always says, 'Tomorrow never comes.'

THE ONLY THING THAT THE GAULS ARE AFRAID OF IS THE SKY FALLING ON THEIR HEADS, AN EVENT WHICH SEEMS IMMINENT AS A TERRIBLE STORM BATTERS THE LITTLE VILLAGE WE KNOW SO WELL.
BRRRAOMM!

ALL THE TOP PEOPLE IN THE VILLAGE HAVE GATHERED TOGETHER IN THE HOUSE OF CHIEF VITALSTATISTIX...
IF ONLY GETAFIX WASN'T AWAY AT THE DRUIDS' ANNUAL CONFERENCE IN THE FOREST OF THE CARNUTES HE'D LOOK AFTER US...

THERE'S NOTHING TO BE AFRAID OF! WE'VE HAD STORMS BEFORE. THIS IS QUITE A BAD ONE, I AGREE, BUT...

SUPPOSE I SING SOMETHING TO BOOST OUR MORALE?

BRRRAOM!

TARANIS, THE GOD OF THUNDER DOESN'T THINK MUCH OF THAT SUGGESTION!
THAT'S ONE GOD WITH HIS HEAD SCREWED ON RIGHT!

AS YOU CAN SEE, THE GAULS ARE CERTAINLY NOT SHORT OF GODS! MORE THAN FOUR HUNDRED RUB SHOULDERS IN THEIR PANTHEON. THERE ARE GODS FOR EVERYTHING: TREES, ROADS, RIVERS. IN FACT, THERE ARE SO MANY THAT WORSHIPPERS SOMETIMES ADDRESS THEM BY CODE NUMBERS TO FACILITATE DELIVERY OF THEIR PRAYERS. FOR INSTANCE, INTELLIGENTSIA, A GODDESS WHOSE SERVICES WERE OFTEN HELD IN SECRET, MAY BE FOUND UNDER M15.

WELL, CHIEF VITALSTATISTIX, AREN'T YOU GOING TO ASK OUR VISITOR IN?
ER... OH... ER... YES...

JUST HOLD THAT A MINUTE
EH?

WHO... WHO ARE YOU?
A TRAVELLER CAUGHT IN THE STORM. GRANT ME THE SHELTER OF YOUR ROOF UNTIL THE WRATH OF THE GODS HAS BEEN APPEASED!

IT LOOKS AS THOUGH THE GODS HAVE HAD A BRAINSTORM UNDER THE INFLUENCE OF THE GODDESS MANIA...

EVER HEARD OF HER?
NO, SHE MUST BE ONE OF THE LUNATIC FRINGE.

COME IN, TRAVELLER. MAKE YOURSELF AT HOME. WHAT CAN WE GET FOR YOU?

HE MUST BE VERY HUNGRY.
I'VE GOT SOME BOAR LEFT, AND A LITTLE GOAT'S MILK.

BRING IT ALL IN. I'LL KEEP HIM COMPANY WHILE HE DRINKS HIS GOAT'S MILK.

SCRUNCH! SCRUNCH!
SCRUNCH! SCRUNCH!

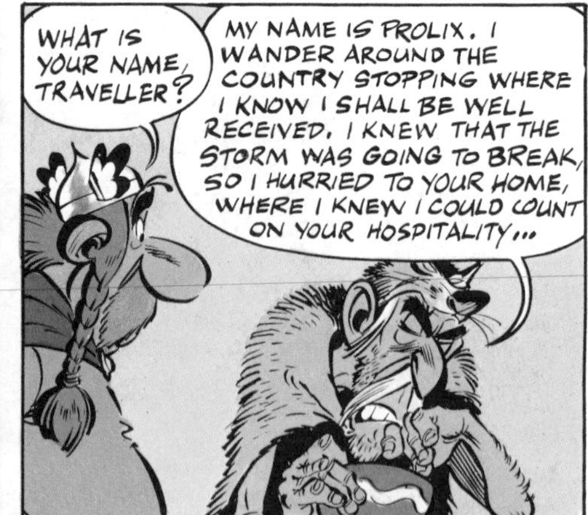
WHAT IS YOUR NAME, TRAVELLER?
MY NAME IS PROLIX. I WANDER AROUND THE COUNTRY STOPPING WHERE I KNOW I SHALL BE WELL RECEIVED. I KNEW THAT THE STORM WAS GOING TO BREAK, SO I HURRIED TO YOUR HOME, WHERE I KNEW I COULD COUNT ON YOUR HOSPITALITY...

... EVEN IF CERTAIN PEOPLE DO HAVE A STRANGE WAY OF SHARING MILK AND BOAR... BUT I KNEW THAT TOO.

H-HOW DID YOU KNOW ALL THAT?

I AM A SOOTHSAYER!
4A

A SOOTHSAYER!?
HO, HO!

BRRRAOOM!

SOMEONE IN THIS ROOM IS SCEPTICAL, AND TARANIS DOESN'T LIKE THAT!

OF COURSE NOT! IT MUST BE THIS IDIOT WHO WAS GOING TO SING! ALL HE DOES IS ANNOY TARANIS!
REALLY... I ASSURE YOU!

PLEASE FORGIVE MY MEN, SOOTHSAYER. THEY SPEND ALL THEIR TIME QUARRELLING.
I KNOW.
4B

ASTERIX'S SCEPTICISM HAS NO EFFECT. SUBJECTED TO THE INFLUENCE OF SO MANY GODS, WHO BOTH PROTECT AND THREATEN THEM, THE NATIONS OF ANTIQUITY WOULD LIKE TO HAVE ADVANCE NOTICE OF THEIR WHIMS. HERE WE MUST INSERT A PARENTHESIS...

IN SHORT, THEY ARE CHARLATANS WHO THRIVE ON CREDULITY, FEAR AND HUMAN SUPERSTITION. HERE WE CLOSE THE PARENTHESIS.

5B

BRRRAOUM!

SOOTHSAYER, SOOTHSAYER! IS THE SKY ABOUT TO FALL ON OUR HEADS?
I SHOULD NEED TO READ THE ENTRAILS OF AN ANIMAL.
YOU COULD TRY A ROAST BOAR.

OBELIX, THERE'S NO MORE BOAR!
AND NOT MUCH READING MATTER LEFT IN THAT ONE EITHER.

THAT DOG WOULD DO... I READ DOGS VERY WELL.
YELLLP!

THE FIRST PERSON TO TOUCH DOGMATIX GETS A BIFF UP THE HOOTER!

WATCH IT! OBELIX'S PREDICTIONS OFTEN WORK OUT!
BONK!

TOO BAD! I SHAN'T BE ABLE TO TELL YOU WHAT THE GODS INTEND.
THE STORM IS GETTING WORSE!

I COULD BRING YOU A FISH. I SELL THEM.

YES, THAT WOULD DO. WE SOOTHSAYERS OFTEN GO TO THE FISHMONGER TO GET SOMETHING TO READ. *
* A TRADITION THAT SURVIVES TO THIS DAY. MODERN FISHMONGERS WRAP THEIR GOODS IN NEWSPAPERS SO THAT CUSTOMERS CAN HAVE SOME READING MATTER.

SOON AFTERWARDS...

BY BORVO, GOD OF SPRINGS, AND BY DAMONA THE HEIFER, AND NO MATTER WHAT THE SCEPTICS THINK, I SEE THAT THE SKY WILL NOT FALL ON YOUR HEADS, AND THAT WHEN THE STORM IS OVER THE WEATHER WILL IMPROVE...

OH! WHAT A RELIEF...
I ALSO SEE THAT THERE'S GOING TO BE A FIGHT.

IF GETAFIX WAS HERE HE'D TELL YOU NOT TO BELIEVE THIS IMPOSTOR! YOU SHOULD BE ASHAMED OF YOURSELF!
BUT, ASTERIX, THE FISH HAS SPOKEN...

THE ONLY THING YOU CAN PREDICT FROM EXAMINING THAT FISH IS THAT ANYONE WHO EATS IT WILL BE ILL!

AND WHY DO YOU THINK THAT, MAY I ASK?
BECAUSE YOUR FISH IS NOT VERY FRESH!

PERHAPS IT WAS A BIT STALE... BUT I'M CERTAIN THAT IF I READ THIS DOG WE SHOULD GET CONFIRMATION OF...

NO ONE HAS EVER READ US, AND NO ONE IS EVER GOING TO!!!

SO YOU THINK MY FISH ISN'T VERY FRESH DO YOU?
WELL, NOT TO PUT TOO FINE A POINT ON IT... NOW IT'S BEEN READ YOU SHOULD CLOSE IT UP AND PUT IT BACK ON THE SLAB...

SPLATCH!

TCHOC!
TCHONC!
TCHAC!
PAF!
PAF
PAF
TCHONC
THONC
BANG!
BANG!
BANG!
WOOF!
WOOF!

BANG!
TCHONC!
PAF PAF PAF PAF PAF PAF PAF

IT'S JUST AS I PREDICTED: NOW THE STORM IS OVER THE WEATHER HAS IMPROVED... NOW I'M LEAVING YOU; OTHERS NEED MY SKILL.

THANK YOU FOR YOUR DELIGHTFUL WELCOME.

GOOD RIDDANCE! I HOPE YOU'LL STOP ACTING LIKE IDIOTS NOW!
8A

BUT, ASTERIX, HE SAID THAT WHEN THE STORM WAS OVER THE WEATHER WOULD IMPROVE...
HE MUST BE CLEVER!

WHAT ABOUT THE FIGHT? HE FORETOLD THE FIGHT!
HE SOON REALISED THAT FIGHTS ARE TWO A SESTERTIUS HERE... ANYWAY, WHENEVER WE DISCUSS YOUR FISH THERE'S BOUND TO BE A FIGHT!

THAT'S JUST NOT TRUE!
ANYWAY, IT WOULDN'T HAPPEN IF THEY WERE FRESH.

SPLOTCH!

IF ONLY I COULD HAVE FORESEEN THAT THEY WERE SO SIMPLE-MINDED... WELL, CHANCE IS A FINE THING, AND I WAS LUCKY! JUST AS I WAS CURSING MYSELF FOR GETTING CAUGHT IN A STORM IN THE MIDDLE OF THE COUNTRYSIDE!
PAFF! BIMM! TCHAC! BOMMM!
8B

GET OUT! EVERYBODY OUT!

I SAID: EVERYBODY OUT!
BUT, DEAREST, THIS IS MY HOME...

OUT!

PHEW! SHE'S HANDY WITH HER BROOM!
ARE WE OUT OF THE DOOR?
YES CHIEF!

TOIIIING!

SOOTHSAYER! SOOTHSAYER! JUST WAIT A MINUTE!

I MUST PLAY THIS CAREFULLY. IN THE LAST VILLAGE, THEY LITERALLY KICKED ME OUT... I MUST ADMIT, THAT LOT WEREN'T STUPID!

SOOTHSAYER, DON'T LEAVE! I WANT TO CONSULT YOU ABOUT MY FUTURE.
NO, NO, NO. THERE ARE SCEPTICS IN YOUR VILLAGE!

THAT LITTLE MAN WITH THE YELLOW MOUSTACHE, AND THE FAT MONSTER WHO WON'T LET ANYONE READ HIS DOG!...
THEY'RE JUST BARBARIANS... YOU MUSTN'T TAKE ANY NOTICE OF THEM. PLEASE STAY!

I FORESEE DIFFICULTIES WITH YOUR BARBARIANS IF I GO BACK TO THE VILLAGE. CAN'T YOU GET THOSE TWO THROWN OUT?
THROW OUT ASTERIX AND OBELIX? WE COULDN'T DO THAT!

OF COURSE, I COULD ALWAYS CAMP IN THIS CLEARING FOR THE TIME BEING...
OH, YES! AND I'LL MAKE SURE ASTERIX AND OBELIX DON'T COME INTO THE FOREST ANY MORE.

I'LL BRING EVERYTHING YOU NEED... THINGS TO EAT...
OH, NO! WE SOOTHSAYERS LEAD A LIFE OF MEDITATION...
10A

JUST BRING ME SOMETHING TO READ: BOARS, DUCKS, CHICKENS, CAKES, BEER...

CAN YOU READ BEER TOO?
IF IT'S WELL KEPT, IT BECOMES VERY LEGIBLE.

YOU CAN HAVE ALL THAT, BUT JUST TELL ME WHAT THE GODS HAVE IN STORE FOR ME...
HMMM...

THE FLIGHT OF THOSE SWALLOWS TELLS ME THAT YOU WILL NOT SPEND ALL YOUR LIFE IN THIS WRETCHED VILLAGE.

BUT MY HUSBAND IS THE CHIEF!
HE WILL BE CALLED TO HIGHER THINGS... I SHALL NEED CUSHIONS AS WELL...

WILL MY RICH BROTHER HOMEOPATHIX TAKE HIM ON AS A BUSINESS PARTNER IN LUTETIA?
I WAS JUST GOING TO SAY SO! NOW LEAVE ME. I MUST MEDITATE.
10B

WHERE ARE YOU GOING?
WE'RE LOOKING FOR WILD BOARS; A BIT OF READING WON'T DO US ANY HARM.
I'M A VORACIOUS READER!

YOU... YOU'RE GOING TO THE FOREST FOR THAT?
WILD BOAR ARE LIKE FUNGI; THEY GROW IN THE FOREST.
BUT THEY'RE ALL GOOD TO EAT, NOT LIKE STUPID OLD FUNGI!

COME ALONG! YOU'RE BOTH INVITED TO DINNER AT MY HOUSE!
?!
?!

I'VE BROUGHT SOME GUESTS HOME, PIGGYWIGGY!

PIGGYWIGGY?... YOU HAVEN'T CALLED ME THAT SINCE WE WERE FIRST MARRIED!

I'VE BEEN WRONG ABOUT YOU, PIGGYWIGGY. I KNOW WE'RE GOING TO BE VERY HAPPY. GET YOUR FRIENDS A BEER WHILE I GET DINNER READY, PIGGY WIGGY.
HGMMMMPFFF!..

WHAT'S THE MATTER WITH YOU TWO?
HAHAHAHA HIHIHIHOHO!
PLEASE FORGIVE US... HEEHEEHEEHOHO! PIGGYWIGGY, OUR CH... HAHAHA!

HGMPFFFFFF!
HAVE YOU QUITE FINISHED?
HA! HA!

MAY I ASK YOU WHY YOU INVITED THESE TWO CLOWNS?
BECAUSE THEY'RE THE BEST WARRIORS IN THE VILLAGE, PIGGYWIGGY!

SINCE OUR DRUID, WHO MAKES THE MAGIC POTION, IS AWAY, WE MUST LOOK AFTER THEM... THE ROMANS COULD ATTACK THE VILLAGE ANY TIME, PIGGYWIGGY...

HUH! THE ROMANS ARE LYING LOW AT THE MOMENT...
YOU NEVER KNOW WITH THEM, PIGGYWIGGY. ASTERIX AND OBELIX SHOULDN'T LEAVE THE VILLAGE TO GO INTO THE FOREST.

BUT WE LIKE GOING INTO THE FOREST!
HGMPF FFFFF

HAHAHAHOHOHI
HIHIHI

OH, SO YOU LIKE GOING INTO THE FOREST, DO YOU? WELL, YOU CAN JUST STAY AND GUARD THE VILLAGE! THAT'S AN ORDER!
HOUHOUHOU!
THAT'S RIGHT, PIGGYWIGGY.
BANG!

YOU CAN EAT HERE EVERY DAY, AND THAT WAY I'LL BE ABLE TO WATCH... ER, LOOK AFTER YOU.
IF THESE IDIOTS ARE GOING TO COME HERE EVERY DAY, THEY'LL HAVE TO CUT OUT THE LAUGHTER!
PRRFFF! PFF! PFF!

LATER...

O SOOTHSAYER, I'VE BROUGHT YOU SOMETHING TO READ ABOUT MY FUTURE IN LUTETIA...

HOW SILLY OF ME! THIS GOOSE IS STUFFED! IT HASN'T GOT ANY ENTRAILS!
IT DOESN'T MATTER; I GET TIRED OF READING TRIPE...

YOU WILL HAVE BEAUTIFUL CLOTHES, THE FINEST HOUSE IN TOWN, AND YOU'LL MIX WITH THE CREAM OF SOCIETY...

SOME TIME LATER...
TRA LA LA LA! TRA LA LA LA!

WHATEVER ARE YOU DOING HERE, IMPEDIMENTA?
ER... UM... I WAS PICKING MUSHROOMS.

YOU DON'T SEEM TO HAVE HAD MUCH LUCK... WOULD YOU LIKE ME TO HELP YOU?

OH, MYOPIA!* I'VE JUST BEEN CONSULTING THE SOOTHSAYER WHO IS CAMPING IN THE FOREST OVER THERE. BUT PLEASE DON'T TELL ANYONE!
* INVOCATION TO GAULISH GODDESS, ACKNOWLEDGING SHORT SIGHTEDNESS

LATER STILL...
... AND DON'T TELL ANYONE, BUT HE TOLD ME THAT GERIATRIX WOULD BECOME VERY RICH, AND I'D HAVE HEAPS OF JEWELS...
UNHYGIENIX

AND STILL LATER...
WHERE ARE YOU OFF TO?
ER... FOR A WALK IN THE FOREST.

WITH THOSE FISH?
OF COURSE. THE POOR CREATURES HAVE A RIGHT TO FRESH AIR, DON'T THEY? YOU MUST ADMIT THEY DON'T OFTEN GO TO THE FOREST.

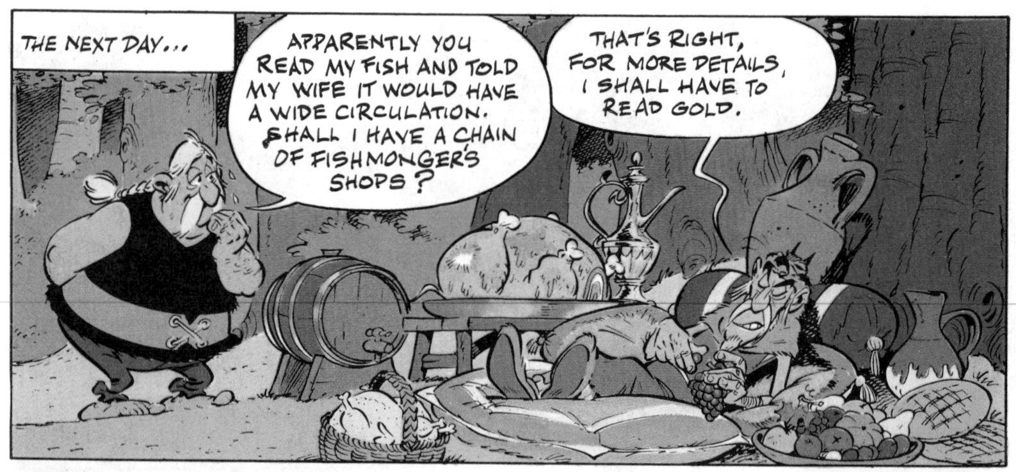
THE NEXT DAY...
APPARENTLY YOU READ MY FISH AND TOLD MY WIFE IT WOULD HAVE A WIDE CIRCULATION. SHALL I HAVE A CHAIN OF FISHMONGER'S SHOPS ?
THAT'S RIGHT, FOR MORE DETAILS, I SHALL HAVE TO READ GOLD.

WOULD SESTERTII DO?
YES, BUT DON'T FORGET THE OFFICIAL RATE OF EXCHANGE: ONE HUNDRED SESTERTII TO THE AURUS*
* GOLD COIN.

HALLO! TAKING YOUR CHICKENS FOR A WALK?
YES...
CLUCK?

14A
WELL, YOUR WIFE TAKES HER FISHES FOR A WALK.
IDIOT!
CLUCK!

ER... I'M JUST GOING FOR A DRINK IN THE FOREST...

THERE ARE SOME FUNNY GOINGS-ON HERE...
WHAT'S GOING ON IS THEY'RE ALL MAKING FOR THE FOREST, AND THEY'RE HAPPY, AND HERE'S ME BORED TO TEARS WITH NOTHING TO DO!

IT'S THE CLOSE SEASON FOR MENHIRS, AND DOGMATIX IS PINING FOR SOME TREES!...
WHERE ARE YOU GOING?

14B
SOME PEOPLE TAKE THEIR FISHES OR THEIR CHICKENS FOR A WALK, I TAKE MY DOG! SO SUCKS TO PIGGYWIGGY!

THIS MAKES A NICE CHANGE FROM THE VILLAGE, DOESN'T IT, DOGMATIX?
WOOF! WOOF!

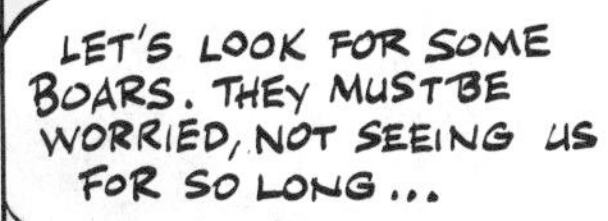
LET'S LOOK FOR SOME BOARS. THEY MUST BE WORRIED, NOT SEEING US FOR SO LONG...

ATTABOY, DOGMATIX! ATTABOY!
SNIFF! SNIFF! SNIFF!

?!?

YELLLP!
?

THERE, THERE, DON'T BE AFRAID... WHAT DID YOU SEE OVER THERE? WE'RE THE ONES WHO FRIGHTEN PEOPLE!

SURE ENOUGH...
?!?

THE MONSTER!
THE DOG READER!

YOU KNOW ASTERIX TOLD YOU NOT TO STAY HERE! COME DOWN, OR I'LL PULL THE TREE UP!
GRRRR!

I SEE A BLONDE GIRL... A VERY PRETTY, YOUNG, BLONDE GIRL... WHO LOVES GREAT WARRIORS WITH RED PIGTAILS...

PIGTAILS?

DID YOU HAVE A GOOD WALK IN THE FOREST ? GET ANY BOARS ?

YES... NO... ER. I DON'T KNOW...
!?!

?

THEY ALL COME BACK FROM THE FOREST COMPLETELY MAD! I MUST GO AND SEE WHAT'S HAPPENING IN THERE!

?

ANYONE AT HOME ?

!!!

WHERE IS HE?
WHERE IS WHO?

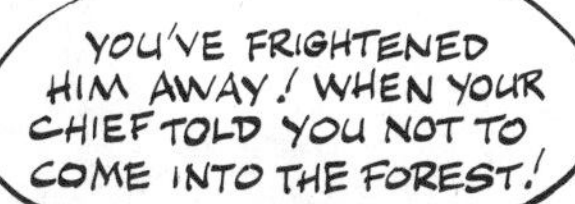

YOU'VE FRIGHTENED HIM AWAY! WHEN YOUR CHIEF TOLD YOU NOT TO COME INTO THE FOREST!

THIS WILL BRING US GREAT MISFORTUNE! THE SOOTHSAYER FORETOLD IT!
THE SOOTHSAYER? IMPEDIMENTA, WAIT FOR ME! ...

ASTERIX HAS DRIVEN THE SOOTHSAYER AWAY!
HE MUST BE MAD! THE SOOTH-SAYER FORETOLD GREAT MISFORTUNES IF HE WAS DRIVEN AWAY!

YOU HAVE DONE A VERY FOOLISH THING, ASTERIX. THE SOOTHSAYER WARNED ME TOO...
OH, SO YOU WENT TO SEE HIM AS WELL...

WELL... ER... ONLY ONCE! FORESIGHT IS ONE OF THE ATTRIBUTES OF A CHIEFTAIN, AND...

HE TOLD ME THE MAN I LOVE WOULD BECOME STRONG AND HANDSOME!
WELL, HE WAS RIGHT THERE, ANYWAY!

NOW LISTEN: IF I'D KNOWN THE SOOTHSAYER WAS IN THE FOREST, I PROBABLY SHOULD HAVE DRIVEN HIM OFF! BUT I DIDN'T KNOW, AND I HAVEN'T THE FAINTEST IDEA WHAT'S GOING ON!
UNHYGIENIX
FISHMONGER
17

THE EXPLANATION IS TO BE FOUND AT THIS VERY MOMENT, IN THE FORTIFIED ROMAN CAMP OF COMPENDIUM...
AVE, CENTURION VOLUPTUOUS ARTERIOSCLEROSUS!
BONK!
AVE. LET'S HAVE YOUR REPORT.

ON PROCEEDING ON PATROL, FOR WHICH YOU GAVE THE ORDERS TO PROCEED WITH, WE FOUND THIS 'ERE INDIVIDUAL IN A CLEARING, AND AFTER A CAUTION HE MADE A STATEMENT WHAT WE WERE NOT VERY SATISFIED WITH.

ARE YOU ONE OF THOSE CRAZY GAULS WHO STILL HOLD OUT AGAINST THE INVADERS?
ME? OH, NO, NO! I DON'T HOLD OUT AGAINST ANYONE!

I'M JUST A SOOTHSAYER.

A SOOTHSAYER? ARE YOU A REAL GAULISH SOOTHSAYER?
OF COURSE... WAIT... I FORESEE THAT YOU WILL BE PROMOTED.
18A

YOU'RE OUT OF LUCK, SOOTHSAYER. WE'VE GOT ORDERS FROM ROME TO ARREST ALL GAULISH SOOTHSAYERS. OUR AUGURERS HAVE WARNED CAESAR THAT GAULISH SOOTHSAYERS ARE A THREAT TO SECURITY...

SO YOU'LL BE SHIPPED OFF TO A MINE IN...
NO, NO, NO! I WAS ONLY JOKING. I'M NOT A REAL SOOTHSAYER, I'M A FAKE.

I TAKE ADVANTAGE OF PEOPLE'S CREDULITY TO LIVE WITHOUT WORKING...
BUT YOU JUST FORETOLD THAT I WOULD BE PROMOTED, ALL THE SAME...

NO, NO, OF COURSE NOT. DON'T BE ABSURD!
JUST WHAT I WAS SAYING...

WHEN I WANT YOUR OPINION I'LL ASK FOR IT, IDIOT! THIS INDIVIDUAL HAS NOT CONVINCED ME! HE IS A SUSPECT!
YES SIR!
18B
BONG!
BONK!

I'M GOING TO TRY YOU OUT TO SEE IF YOU ARE A REAL SOOTHSAYER ...

SAY A NUMBER BETWEEN I AND XII
ER... VII

PHEW! I'M QUITE SAFE. I'VE NEVER BEEN LUCKY AT GAMBLING.

YOU WIN. CHAIN HIM UP. I KNEW HE WAS A REAL SOOTHSAYER WHEN HE SAID I'D GET PROMOTION.

NO! IF I WERE A REAL SOOTHSAYER, I SHOULD HAVE KNOWN THAT THE DICE WOULD MAKE VII, SO I WOULD HAVE SAID VIII, AND THEN YOU WOULDN'T HAVE BELIEVED I WAS A REAL SOOTHSAYER BECAUSE THE DICE SAID VII AND NOT VIII!

O CENTURION, I DIDN'T UNDERSTAND A WORD HE JUST SAID. DO WE LOCK HIM UP?

I'M AN IMPOSTOR! I FLATTERED THE PEOPLE OF THAT VILLAGE TO MAKE THEM BELIEVE ME! THEY'RE SO SIMPLE-MINDED THEY BELIEVE ANYTHING I TELL THEM, AND...
... THE BELIEVE ANYTHING YOU TELL THEM? WELL NOW, COULD YOU FRIGHTEN THEM? PERSUADE THEM TO LEAVE THEIR VILLAGE?
AS SURE AS V AND II MAKE VII!

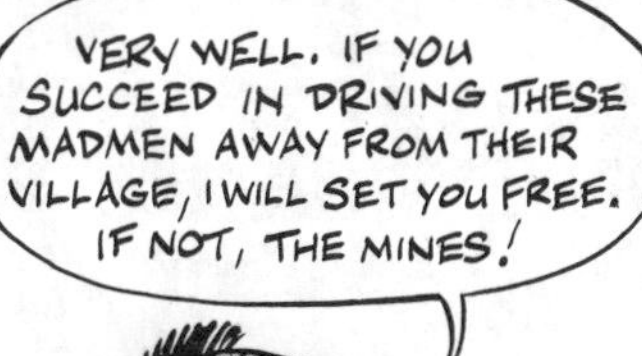
VERY WELL. IF YOU SUCCEED IN DRIVING THESE MADMEN AWAY FROM THEIR VILLAGE, I WILL SET YOU FREE. IF NOT, THE MINES!

OFF YOU GO, AND DON'T TRY TO RUN AWAY!
HE'S A FRAUD, THEN, IS HE, THAT BLOKE YOU WAS ARGUING WITH?

NO, NO! HE'S A REAL SOOTHSAYER, BUT HE'S GOING TO WORK FOR US!

YOU DID A VERY SILLY THING THERE, ASTERIX! IT IS DANGEROUS TO CROSS A SOOTHSAYER!
THAT IMPOSTOR TOOK YOUR GOLD, LIVED OFF YOUR FOOD AND DRINK, AND NOW HE'S SIMPLY GONE OFF TO LOOK FOR SOME MORE STUPID PEOPLE!

WELL, I DON'T THINK HE WAS AN IMPOSTOR. I DON'T LIKE HIS CHOICE OF READING MATTER, BUT SOME OF WHAT HE SAID WAS RIGHT.
OH NO, OBELIX! NOT YOU TOO!

FOR ONCE YOUR FAT FRIEND HAS SAID SOMETHING SENSIBLE...
I AM NOT FAT! I'M A GREAT WARRIOR WITH RED PIGTAILS.

LOOK!

THE SOOTHSAYER! THE SOOTHSAYER IS BACK!

YES, I AM BACK TO TELL YOU THAT MISFORTUNE IS UPON YOU, GAULS! YOUR VILLAGE IS CURSED BY THE GODS!

THE VERY AIR YOU BREATHE WILL COME FROM THE DEPTHS OF HELL. IT WILL BE FOUL, POISONED, AND YOUR FACES WILL TURN A GHASTLY HUE...

FLEE! FLEE, RASH PEOPLE! IT IS YOUR ONLY CHANCE OF SURVIVAL! DON'T SAY I DIDN'T WARN YOU!
20

SO NOW WHAT DO WE DO?
SCRATCH SCRATCH!
I'M NOT STAYING IN THIS ACCURSED VILLAGE A MOMENT LONGER! LET'S SET OFF FOR LUTETIA, PIGGYWIGGY! I'M SURE THAT A GREAT FUTURE AWAITS...
YOU'RE ALL MAD! YOU'RE NEVER GOING TO LEAVE THE VILLAGE ON ACCOUNT OF THAT FRAUD!?!
POC POC POC

HE IS NOT A FRAUD! I AM THE LIVING PROOF OF IT!
DID YOU SAY LIVING...?

YES, SIR! I'M GETTING YOUNGER AND STRONGER EVERY DAY!
WE CAN FIGHT AGAINST THE ROMANS, BUT NOT AGAINST THE WILL OF THE GODS!

WHERE CAN WE GO? THE SOOTHSAYER TOLD ME I'D HAVE A CHAIN OF FISH-MONGERS' SHOPS IN THIS AREA! I'LL HAVE TO STAY SOMEWHERE NEAR!

LET'S GO AND CAMP ON THE LITTLE ISLAND JUST OFF THE COAST!
BUT, PIGGYWIGGY, LUTETIA IS WHERE...
!

THEN, WHEN THE ANGER OF THE GODS IS APPEASED, WE CAN COME BACK TO THE VILLAGE... AGREED?
I'M STAYING!

EVERYONE TO THE BEACH!

ARE YOU GOING TOO, OBELIX?
WELL... ER...

OH, VERY WELL, I'LL STAY!

LAUNCH THE BOATS!

COME ON, BOYS! WE'RE GOING ON BOARD!

ARE YOU ALL RIGHT, GERIATRIX, MY LOVE?
GLUG, GLUG, GLUG!

DO YOU REALLY THINK THE SOOTHSAYER IS HAVING US ON?
I'M SURE OF IT! I DON'T KNOW WHAT HE TOLD YOU, BUT THE BEST THING TO DO WOULD BE TO LAUGH IT OFF.

I DON'T FEEL MUCH LIKE LAUGHING.
LET'S GO AND HIDE IN THE FOREST AND SEE WHAT HAPPENS NEXT.

MEANWHILE...
THERE YOU ARE! THEY'VE LEFT, JUST LIKE I TOLD YOU THEY WOULD.
I NEVER DOUBTED IT. YOU SOOTHSAYERS HAVE GREAT POWERS.
RIGHT. DO WE LOCK HIM UP?

YOU PROMISED ME MY LIBERTY! I'M NOT A SOOTHSAYER! I'M A CON MAN, THAT'S ALL!

LET'S GO OFF TO THE VILLAGE AND CHECK UP ON THESE STATEMENTS OF YOURS.

...SO THEN I GOT THE IDEA OF GOING ON ABOUT THE FOUL AIR, BECAUSE, YOU SEE, I LIVE NEAR A TANNERY IN LUTETIA, SO...
OH, SO IT WASN'T A GENUINE PREDICTION?

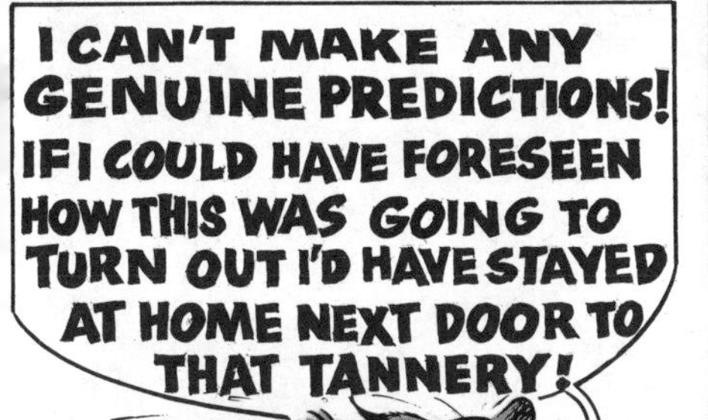
I CAN'T MAKE ANY GENUINE PREDICTIONS! IF I COULD HAVE FORESEEN HOW THIS WAS GOING TO TURN OUT I'D HAVE STAYED AT HOME NEXT DOOR TO THAT TANNERY!

SSH... WE'RE NEAR THE VILLAGE... ALL SEEMS QUIET, BUT YOU NEVER KNOW WITH THOSE GAULS!

WE NEED A SCOUT TO GO ON AHEAD. I WANT A VOLUNTEER.
SIR!

AND YOU CAN TAKE THE SOOTHSAYER WITH YOU.
I KNEW IT.

I KNOW.
NO, YOU DON'T! NO YOU DON'T!
DO WE LOCK HIM UP, THEN?
23

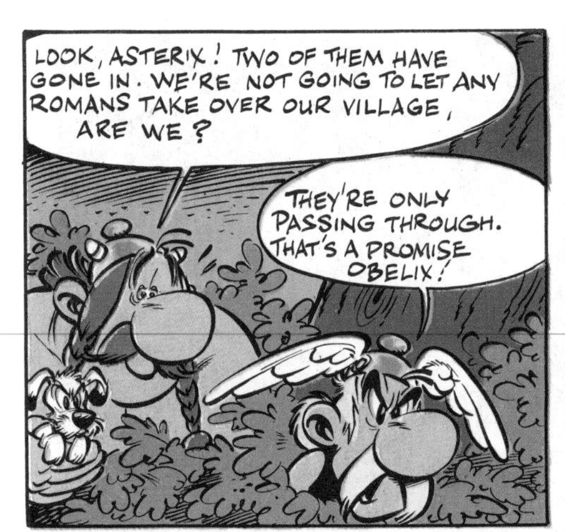
LOOK, ASTERIX! TWO OF THEM HAVE GONE IN. WE'RE NOT GOING TO LET ANY ROMANS TAKE OVER OUR VILLAGE, ARE WE?
THEY'RE ONLY PASSING THROUGH. THAT'S A PROMISE OBELIX!

ALL CLEAR.

ER... CENTURION... DO YOU THINK THIS IS REALLY WISE? IT COULD BE AN AMBUSH... YOU KNOW WHAT THESE GAULS ARE LIKE...
NO, NO, MY GOOD FELLOW! SOOTHSAYERS ARE NEVER WRONG, YOU KNOW! RIGHT, FORWARD MARCH, IV ABREAST!

THE LIBERATION OF A CITY IS ALWAYS A MOVING EXPERIENCE!
24A

EMPTY, DESERTED AND UNINHABITED, AS YOU MIGHT SAY, O CENTURION!
UNHYG

YOU ARE TO START FOR ROME, BEARING A MESSAGE FOR CAESAR. YOU WILL TELL HIM: "ALL GAUL IS OCCUPIED." HE WILL ASK "ALL?" YOU WILL REPLY: "ALL!" HE WILL UNDERSTAND.

YOU'LL BE SURE TO GET PROMOTION, SIR, SAME AS THIS 'ERE SOOTHSAYER WAS SOOTHSAYING!
OF COURSE.
NO! I NEVER! I NEVER SAID ANY SUCH THING!

OH? AND WHY NOT? HAVE THE GODS SHOWN YOU SOMETHING NASTY IN MY FUTURE THEN?
I TELL YOU, I DON'T KNOW A THING ABOUT IT!

ANSWER ME, OR I'LL HAVE YOU OPENED UP SO YOU CAN READ YOUR OWN ENTRAILS!
NO! NO! YOU'LL GET PROMOTION ALL RIGHT!
DO WE LOCK HIM UP, THEN?
24B

WE CAN'T LEAVE THEM IN OUR VILLAGE, ASTERIX. LET'S GET IN THERE, ALL THREE OF US, AND THROW THEM OUT!
NO! WE ARE GOING TO TEACH THEM ALL A LESSON: THE ROMANS, THE SOOTHSAYER, AND EVEN OUR OWN PEOPLE!

DON'T YOU WORRY, OBELIX. THERE'LL BE ANOTHER BANQUET IN OUR VILLAGE YET! YOU MARK MY WORDS!

HULLO, BOYS! HUNTING BOARS?
?
?

OUR DRUID, GETAFIX!
LOOK AT THAT, BOYS! I WON THE GOLDEN CAULDRON FOR THE DRUID OF THE YEAR AT OUR ANNUAL CONFERENCE IN THE FOREST OF THE CARNUTES!

AND A VERY INTERESTING CONFERENCE IT WAS. THE DRUID STATISTIX HAS BEEN FIGURING OUT SOME FUTURE TRENDS IN OUR PROFESSION...

IS SOMETHING WRONG, BOYS?
I'LL TELL YOU ALL ABOUT IT, O DRUID...

SOON AFTERWARDS...
HMM... FOUL AIR, EH? A GHASTLY HUE, EH?

I BROUGHT A FEW RATHER AMUSING LITTLE INGREDIENTS HOME WITH ME... PASS ME DOWN THAT BEAUTIFUL CAULDRON...

SPLENDID, SPLENDID... THE WIND'S JUST ABOUT TO CHANGE. THERE IS NOT A MOMENT TO LOSE.

A SOOTHSAYER MIGHT ALWAYS COME IN USEFUL ...
WHAT I ALWAYS SAY IS, ORDERS IS ORDERS, AND IF THIS IS ONE OF THEM SOOTHSAYERS 'E'S GOT TO BE LOCKED UP, SIR.

LISTEN, I WARNED THEM ABOUT THE FOUL AIR IN THE VILLAGE... NOW, CAN YOU SMELL ANYTHING NASTY ?

MEANWHILE ...
CAN I HAVE A TASTE ?

NO, OBELIX, YOU CANNOT!

OUT OF THE WAY, BOYS! GET ROUND TO THE WINDWARD SIDE, QUICK !
PSSCHCH!

NO! OBELIX, DON'T!
SNIFF! SNIFF! SNIFF!

YOU KNOW, WE NEVER STOOP TO WORD-PLAY, ASTERIX, BUT IF WE DID I MIGHT VENTURE TO SAY THAT THIS IS THE POLLUTION TO ALL OUR PROBLEMS !

TARANIS, THE GOD OF STORMS AND THUNDER, IS IN MELLOW MOOD, AND SENDS A GENTLE BREEZE, WAFTING THROUGH THE AIR A SMELL WHICH WAS STILL UNFAMILIAR IN THE YEAR 50 BC...
YUK!

I SAY, DO YOU SMELL A FUNNY KIND OF SMELL, ALL OF A SUDDEN?
SNIFF! SNIFF!

A FUNNY KIND OF SMELL?
YES, A FUNNY KIND OF SMELL.
IT'S A BIT LIKE WHERE I LIVE IN ROME.
SNIFF! SNIFF!

YOU LIVE NEAR A TANNERY, I SUPPOSE?

YES! HE GOT IT RIGHT! HE IS A SOOTHSAYER!

OooooH... CENTURION!

THE AIR IN THIS VILLAGE ISN'T FIT TO BREATHE... IT'S PESTILENTIAL, THAT'S WHAT IT IS!

SNIFF! SNIFF!
PES... PESTILENTIAL?
YOU TAKE MY WORD FOR IT. I'M A VETERAN, I AM. I'VE KNOWN PLENTY OF CAMPS AND BARRACKS, BUT I NEVER SMELT ANYTHING LIKE THIS BEFORE!

?!?

AMAZING! IT'S LIKE MAGIC! EVEN THE GODS OBEY YOU!
BUT IT'S NOT POSSIBLE!! IT JUST ISN'T POSSIBLE!

TRUMPETER! SOUND THE ASSEMBLY! WE'RE GOING TO EVACUATE THIS DAMNED VILLAGE. THE GODS HAVE CURSED IT!

OH NO! IF I GO BLOWING THIS SOMETHING HORRIBLE MIGHT HAPPEN!
28A

TANTANTARAUGHUGHUGHUGH!

THE PROPHECY HAS COME TRUE! HE REALLY IS A SOOTHSAYER!

28B
THERE! WHAT DID I TELL YOU?

I FORGOT MY LYRE, SO I WENT BACK TO THE VILLAGE TO GET IT, AND I FOUND MYSELF BREATHING FOUL AIR... AIR FROM THE DEPTHS OF HELL! EVEN THE ROMANS HAD TO RUN FOR IT!

YOU SEE? YOU SEE? WE SHOULD HAVE GONE TO LUTETIA, LIKE THE SOOTHSAYER SAID! YOU STUPID GREAT BOAR!
DARLING... AREN'T I YOUR PIGGY WIGGY ANY MORE?

WELL, I'LL JUST HAVE TO DO WITHOUT MY LYRE.

O, I DO LIKE TO BE BESIDE THE LITUS...

TCHOUF!

ARE YOU CRAZY? COME BACK!
I'D RATHER BREATHE FOUL AIR THAN LISTEN TO THAT!
WHAT ARE YOU SINGING FOR? ANYWAY?
THE SOOTHSAYER TOLD ME VOICES LIKE MINE WERE GOING TO BE VERY POPULAR IN THE FUTURE. I'M PRACTISING.

WELL, ALL WE HAVE TO DO NOW IS WAIT FOR FRESH AIR TO DISPERSE THE BAD SMELL IN THE VILLAGE, AND THEN WE'LL GO AND LOOK FOR OUR FRIENDS...

AND AS FOR THE ROMANS, I'M COUNTING ON YOU. YOU'RE SURE TO THINK OF SOMETHING.
I'VE THOUGHT OF SOMETHING ALREADY. WE GO TO THEIR CAMP AND BASH THE WHOLE PLACE UP.

WHEREVER DO YOU GET ALL THESE ORIGINAL IDEAS?
A HANDSOME WARRIOR WITH RED PIGTAILS, YES! BUT I'M NOT JUST A PRETTY FACE!

I OUGHT TO HAVE YOU ARRESTED, BUT YOU MIGHT COME IN USEFUL TO ME IN MY FUTURE CAREER... WITH THE HELP OF YOUR PREDICTIONS AND ADVICE I COULD GO FAR! I MIGHT EVEN RISE TO THE POSITION OF ...

AND YOU WILL NOT FIND ME UNGRATEFUL.
BUT REMEMBER, IF YOU ARE NOT A REAL SOOTHSAYER, IF YOU'VE BEEN HAVING ME ON, I WILL NEVER FORGIVE YOU!!!

30B

I JUST CAN'T MAKE HEAD OR TAIL OF IT... HAVE I TURNED INTO A REAL SOOTHSAYER?

AND ANYWAY, I DO WISH THEY'D ALL GIVE UP GRABBING ME BY THE FRONT OF MY...

SAY A NUMBER FROM I TO XII!
CLICK! CLICK! CLICK!
GLUG!

ER... ALL RIGHT.. VIII

PSST!
?

CAREFUL! WE DON'T WANT ANYONE BUT ME TO KNOW YOU'RE A REAL SOOTHSAYER... BUT YOU WERE JUST A LITTLE TOO CLEVER THERE. EVEN THAT FOOL MIGHT SUSPECT SOMETHING...

I... I FEEL A BIT WEAK...

WHAT I ASK MYSELF IS, NOW WHERE AM I?
CAN I HELP YOU?

NO. YOU DON'T KNOW, EVEN LESS THAN WHAT I DO, BECAUSE I'M AN OPTIONE AND YOU'RE JUST A COMMON LEGIONARY.
IDIOT!

MEANWHILE...
SPLOSH! SPLOSH! SPLOCH!

GETAFIX! YOU'RE BACK AT LAST!

MAYBE YOU CAN APPEASE THE ANGER OF THE GODS, WHICH HAS FALLEN UPON OUR POOR VILLAGE...
NONSENSE! YOU'RE VICTIMS OF YOUR OWN CREDULITY, THAT'S ALL!

OH, WAIT A MINUTE GETAFIX! I'VE SEEN THE VILLAGE! I'VE BREATHED THE FOUL AIR, STRAIGHT FROM THE DEPTHS OF HELL! I'VE SEEN THE ROMANS GO GREEN!
THAT'S RIGHT! OUR BARD MAY HAVE A VOICE LIKE A SISTRUM*, BUT HE DOESN'T TELL LIES.
* A KIND OF METAL RATTLE.

YOU KNOW WHAT YOUR BARD HAS TO SAY TO YOU IN HIS VOICE LIKE A SISTRUM?

CALM DOWN, CALM DOWN! I'LL GIVE YOU A LITTLE DEMONSTRATION OF THE ANGER OF THE GODS.

OBELIX! EMPTY THAT CAULDRON AND...

...BRING IT OVER HERE.
THERE YOU ARE!

SOON AFTERWARDS...
VERY GOOD! NOW, ALL OF YOU GO OVER THERE, THE WAY THE WIND'S BLOWING.

HOLD IT!

PSSCHCHCH!

BY TOUTATIS! I CAN'T STAND THIS!
?
STOP IT, BY BELENOS! STOP IT!
OOOOH!

WHAT ON EARTH IS THE MATTER WITH YOU?
CHIEF, DO YOU THINK YOU COULD LOWER YOURSELF TO THE LEVEL OF OUR PROBLEMS FOR A MOMENT?

THERE YOU ARE, THAT'S THE ANGER OF THE GODS: A CONCOCTION IN A CAULDRON!

THE SMELL DOESN'T SEEM TO BOTHER YOU ALL THAT MUCH..
HUH, WELL, WHAT WITH HIS FISH...

SPLATCH!

I EXPECT YOU KNOW WHAT TO DO NOW?
I THINK SO, GETAFIX...

WE GO BACK TO THE VILLAGE TONIGHT. IN PEACE AND QUIET!

AND THAT VERY NIGHT...
DROP ANCHOR!

DON'T YOU THINK IT'S A BIT DANGEROUS TO ANCHOR IN BETWEEN THE GAULISH COAST AND THIS UNKNOWN ISLAND, CAP'N?
SHIVER ME TIMBERS, NO! WE CONSULTED THE ENTRAILS OF A MACKEREL, AND THE ORACLE WAS ABSOLUTELY POSITIVE: IT'S SAFE AS HOUSES TO ANCHOR HERE OVERNIGHT.
34A

NEXT MORNING...
THIS IS TERRIBLE! A SHOAL OF GAULS HAS CROSSED OUR PATH!
GLUG! GLUG! GLUG! GLUG! GLUG!

I'VE HAD A BELLYFUL OF ENTRAILS!
STOP BELLYACHING! I THOUGHT YOU HAD MORE GUTS!

34B

I MUST SAY, IT'S NICE TO BE HOME!
WELL, I MUST SAY I THINK WE'D HAVE BEEN BETTER OFF IN LUTETIA, LIKE THE SOOTHSAYER SAID.

BUT HE WASN'T REALLY A SOOTHSAYER!
WHAT MAKES YOU SO SURE?

I'VE BEEN TALKING TO GERIATRIX'S WIFE AND TO BACTERIA, AND THEY'RE NOT CONVINCED. THAT'S WHY I THOUGHT LUTETIA MIGHT BE THE PLACE...

GETAFIX, THE WOMEN AREN'T CONVINCED THAT HE'S A FRAUD...
OF COURSE THEY'RE NOT. HE ONLY FORETOLD PLEASANT THINGS FOR THEM, SUCH AS THEIR HUSBANDS BECOMING HANDSOME AND INTELLIGENT...
35A

SUPPOSE WE GAVE THAT SOOTHSAYER A SURPRISE?

ASTERIX, I'M PROUD OF YOU! IF WE GIVE THE SOOTHSAYER A SURPRISE THAT WILL PROVE THAT HE'S NOT REALLY A SOOTHSAYER!
OH, SO YOU THINK I NEED TO BECOME HANDSOME AND INTELLIGENT, DO YOU?

YOU ARRANGE A LITTLE SURPRISE, ASTERIX! I'M OFF TO MAKE SOME MAGIC POTION!

SOON AFTERWARDS...
WELL, ARE WE ALL AGREED? IF THE SOOTHSAYER DOESN'T GUESS WHAT'S IN STORE FOR HIM, WILL YOU BELIEVE THAT HE ISN'T A REAL SOOTHSAYER?
35B

INCLUDING US GIRLS?
SPECIALLY YOU GIRLS!
OH, I LOVE SURPRISES!

I'VE NEVER TASTED YOUR FAMOUS MAGIC POTION...

MM... NOT BAD... MYSELF, I'D HAVE ADDED ANOTHER PINCH OF SALT...

AND DOES IT REALLY WORK?
HAVE A GO!
36A

BIFF!

CLUCK?

I-AM-NOT-IN-FAVOUR-OF-WOMEN'S-LIB!
POF! POF! POF!

COME ON, ALL! WE'RE OFF TO THE FORTIFIED CAMP OF COMPENDIUM!
AND LET'S HOPE THE GODS ARE NOT PROTECTING PROLIX THE SOOTHSAYER!
36B

YOU, GAUL! THE CENTURION WANTS YOU IN HIS TENT.
NOT AGAIN!

AH, SOOTHSAYER! TELL ME ABOUT MY FUTURE!
FLOP!
BUT I'VE TOLD IT ALL ALREADY: THE GODS WILL PROTECT YOU, YOU'LL GET PROMOTION, YOU'LL...

I KNOW, I KNOW, BUT TELL ME WHAT IT WILL BE LIKE WHEN I'M CAESAR.

WELL, YOU'LL BE VERY POWERFUL AND THE COMMON PEOPLE WILL FEAR YOU...
EXCELLENT, EXCELLENT... AND HOW ABOUT CLEOPATRA?

CLEOPATRA? WHAT DO YOU MEAN, CLEOPATRA?

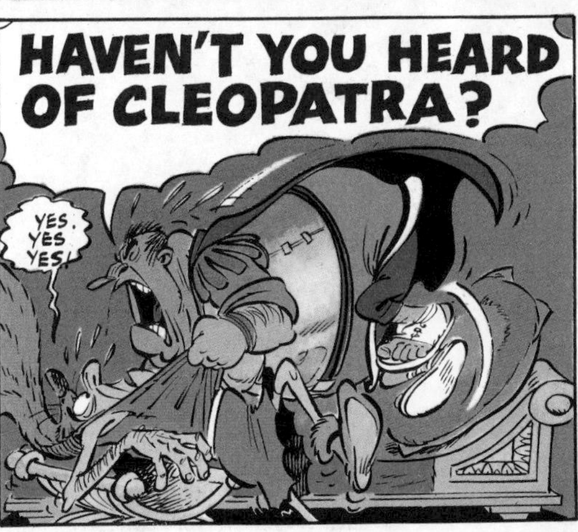

HAVEN'T YOU HEARD OF CLEOPATRA?
YES, YES, YES!

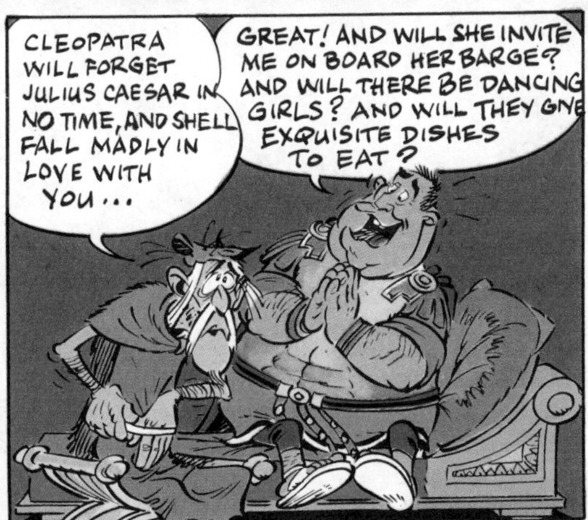

CLEOPATRA WILL FORGET JULIUS CAESAR IN NO TIME, AND SHE'LL FALL MADLY IN LOVE WITH YOU...
GREAT! AND WILL SHE INVITE ME ON BOARD HER BARGE? AND WILL THERE BE DANCING GIRLS? AND WILL THEY GIVE EXQUISITE DISHES TO EAT?

YES, YES, THEY'LL GIVE YOU... THEY'LL GIVE YOU PRE-SERVED PIGS' EARS.
PRESERVED PIGS' EARS? SOOTHSAYER, YOU'RE A MARVEL!

AND WHILE THE UNSUSPECTING ROMANS ARE LIVING IN A FOOL'S PARADISE, NEAR THE CAMP...
WAIT HERE, AND DON'T MAKE ANY NOISE. OBELIX AND I WILL SEE TO THE SENTRIES.

SSSH!
?

HEY, ASTERIX, HE SAID IT WASN'T SURPRISING. DO YOU THINK THE SOOTH-SAYER HAD WARNED THEM?

DON'T MAKE MATTERS MORE COMPLICATED! GO AND TELL THE OTHERS THEY CAN COME IN.

THE GAULS!!!

GAULS INSIDE THE CAMP, AND YOU DIDN'T WARN ME?!!
BUT HOW WAS I TO KNOW?

LEAVE HIM TO ME!
?

HOW WERE YOU TO KNOW? YOU MEAN TO SAY YOU MADE UP ALL THAT ABOUT LUTETIA, AND PIGGYWIGGY GO-ING INTO PARTNERSHIP WITH MY BROTHER?

GOOD SHOT MADAM!
PAFF!
39A

PAFF!
CHARGE!
THAT WAS MY LITTLE 'PEDIMENTA' THAT WAS!
ZZWWIP!

NO WOMEN ALLOWED IN CAMP! NO WOMEN ALLOWED IN CAMP!
BUT, MY DEAR MADAM, WHAT DO YOU WANT WITH ME?
39B

YOU'RE... YOU'RE JUST WONDERFUL... WE HAVE HEAPS OF THINGS IN COMMON...
TOC!
PAF!

COME ALONG, OBELIX. THIS IS NO TIME FOR A ROMULUS AND REMUS ACT.*
* ALLUSION TO THE FAMOUS ROMAN WOLF.

WE CAN GO HOME NOW. I THINK OUR LITTLE DEMONSTRATION WAS QUITE A SUCCESS.

OH, SO THAT WAS A LITTLE DEMONSTRATION, WAS IT?

YOU WERE RIGHT, ASTERIX. THAT FRAUD OF A SOOTHSAYER WAS PLAYING ON OUR CREDULITY. BUT IT WON'T HAPPEN AGAIN.
I WONDER IF MAGIC POTION IS FATTENING?

WHO ARE YOU, ROMAN? AND WHAT DO YOU THINK YOU'RE DOING IN MY VILLAGE?
WELL... ER... THAT IS TO SAY...

ALL RIGHT, ALL RIGHT! I'VE HAD ABOUT ENOUGH ROMANS FOR ONE DAY. THROW THESE TWO OUT FOR ME!

OH, SO YOU WEREN'T TO KNOW, EH? SO YOU'RE NOT A REAL SOOTHSAYER AFTER ALL! SO YOU'VE BEEN HAVING ME ON!

ARE WE DISTURBING YOU?
?

BONG!

AND WHO ARE YOU?
BULBUS CROCUS, SPECIAL ENVOY FROM JULIUS CAESAR, THAT'S WHO I AM.

YOU SENT A MESSAGE TO ROME, CENTURION, SAYING THAT ALL GAUL WAS OCCUPIED. ALL? ALL!

THE MESSENGER! I'D FORGOTTEN ALL ABOUT HIM!
WELL, JULIUS CAESAR TOLD ME TO CHECK UP ON THIS STATEMENT OF YOURS AND GO AND SEE IF YOU REALLY HAD CONQUERED THE REBEL GAULS...
PAF!

AND LOOK WHAT YOUR CONQUERED GAULS DID TO US, BY JUPITER!

IT'S NOT MY FAULT! IT WAS THAT FRAUD OF A SOOTHSAYER WHO...

SILENCE! YOU'RE DEMOTED TO THE RANKS!

YOU'RE NOT A CENTURION ANY MORE, YOU'RE A COMMON LEGIONARY, AND EVEN THAT'S TOO GOOD FOR YOU!

OH, SO I'M GOING TO GET PROMOTION, AM I? OPTIONE, ARREST THIS IMPOSTOR!

IF THIS 'ERE PERSON IS NOT A SOOTHSAYER, I GOT NO REASON TO ARREST HIM!

BUT OF COURSE HE'S A SOOTHSAYER! NO DOUBT ABOUT IT! A GREAT GAULISH SOOTHSAYER, PROTECTED BY THE GODS, AND...

I DON'T TAKE NO ORDERS FROM A COMMON LEGIONARY! YOU GO AND SWEEP OUT THE CAMP! ON YOUR OWN! AND NO COMPLAINTS!

AND JUST SPEAK PROPER TO A SUPERIOR OFFICER!
ER... AND... WHAT ARE YOU GOING TO DO WITH ME?

OUT! NO CIVILIANS ALLOWED INSIDE THIS CAMP!

THE GODS KNOW WHAT TOMORROW MAY BRING, BUT I'M THROUGH WITH SOOTHSAYING!

AND IF EVER I CHANGE MY MIND, MAY TARANIS MAKE THE SKY FALL ON MY HEAD!

BRAOUM!

HOWEVER, THE ANGER OF TARANIS IS SHORT-LIVED...

...AND SOON TOUTATIS IS MAKING THE SUN SHINE DOWN ON THE VILLAGE, AT PEACE ONCE AGAIN.

WELL, OBELIX, OLD FRIEND, I DON'T KNOW WHAT THE SOOTH-SAYER SAID TO YOU, BUT I'M SURE YOU'LL BE HAPPY!

YOU'RE NOT A SOOTHSAYER, ASTERIX.
OH, AREN'T I? DIDN'T I TELL YOU THERE'D BE ANOTHER BANQUET IN THIS VILLAGE... WELL SO THERE WILL BE, THIS VERY EVENING!

HOW RIGHT YOU ARE! YOU DID FORETELL IT!

ARE THERE GOING TO BE BOARS?
LOTS OF BOARS! I CAN SEE THEM NOW!
?

ASTERIX!
?

OF COURSE, I DON'T BELIEVE ANY OF THAT NONSENSE, BUT... DO YOU THINK WE'LL SOON BE GOING TO LUTETIA WITH PIGGY... WITH VITALSTATISTIX?

HOPELESS! ASTERIX, THEY'RE HOPELESS!
44A

BUT THAT EVENING ALL IS FORGIVEN AND FORGOTTEN. UNDER THE STARS AND THE PROTECTION OF TOUTATIS, GOD OF THE TRIBE, ROSMERTA, THE GODDESS OF PLENTY, AND CERNUNNOS, THE GOD OF NATURE, THE GAULS, UNITED ONCE AGAIN, ENJOY THE PRESENT AND TAKE NO THOUGHT FOR THE FUTURE.
THE END
UDERZO & GOSCINNY
8.72
44B